For my best friend,
and mentor, wife, Rhonda D.L .

Library of Congress Cataloging-in-Publication Data

Legge, David, 1963–
    Bamboozled / David Legge.
        p.   cm.
    Summary: A young girl on her weekly visit to her grandad feels
    that there is something out of the ordinary but can't figure out
    what it is.
    ISBN 0-590-47989-X
    [1. Grandfathers — Fiction. 2. Family life — Fiction.] I. Title.
    PZ7.L52128Bam   1994
    [E] — dc20   94-18647
                                                                CIP
                                                                 AC

12 11 10 9 8 7 6 5 4 3 2 1   5 6 7 8 9/9 0/0

Printed in Hong Kong

First printing, March 1995

The illustrations in this book were painted in watercolors

BAMBOOZLED

DAVID LEGGE

SCHOLASTIC INC.

New York

I love my grandpa.
I visit him every week.
And every week, things are
the same.
But *last* week when I arrived,
something seemed odd.

We sat down, as usual, and talked for a while. Then Grandpa poured two cups of tea, and we ate fresh pastries he'd bought that morning.

We played cards.

As always, he won.

We looked at his old
photo albums, and I listened
to his stories about
the good old days.

I helped him with the
housework, but something
still bothered me.

We worked in the garden, and I
planted bulbs in the flower bed.

I pushed the wheelbarrow while
Grandpa pruned the roses.
But still, something seemed odd.
It was on the tip of my tongue . . . .

"You *are* quiet today," Grandpa said as he fed the cat.

"I know," I said.
"I can't figure it out.
There's something I can't put
my finger on. Something,
today, seems odd."

"Well — I've redecorated the hallway."

No, it wasn't that.

"I've bought two new fish."

No, it wasn't that either.

Then, just as we were saying
good-bye on the doorstep,
it suddenly hit me.

"Grandpa!" I said. "That's what it is.

Your socks are odd — they don't match!"

Silly Grandpa.

We laughed and laughed!